RU

Queen of
EDINBURGH CASTLE

Story by
John Millar

Illustrated by
Jenni Meechan

After coming top in a school history exam, Ruby's prize was an outing with her classmates to Edinburgh Castle.

When Ruby set off, with her classmates and their teacher, Miss Laird, there was a surprise.

Miss Laird produced a crown and placed it on Ruby's head.

'Now you are Queen Ruby of Edinburgh Castle,' she said and the other pupils clapped and cheered as Ruby adjusted her crown.

Ruby was fascinated by the castle. At school she had learned the castle sat on top of an extinct volcano and had been built there because it towered over the area and was easy to defend from attack.

Edinburgh Castle was very old. It had been a royal castle since the days of King David I, who was crowned in 1124. The king's mother, Queen Margaret was made a saint. In her memory King David had a chapel built... St Margaret's Chapel which is Edinburgh's oldest building and even today marriages and christenings are held there.

As the pupils were led up Castlehill, Ruby was thinking about all the sights, like the 15th century Mons Meg cannon...

...The Half Moon Battery — the mighty cannons standing on the ruins of David's Tower. Work began to create the battery and improve castle defences after The Lang Siege, an attack on the castle that lasted two years and ended in 1573.

... the ornate hammerbeam roof of the Great Hall commissioned by James IV, and made from wood shipped from Norway.

... and, of course the Honours Of Scotland, the nation's crown jewels and Britain's oldest royal regalia.

'I almost forgot the Stone of Destiny, the ancient stone used at the coronation of Scotland's monarchs,' Ruby said to herself.

Ruby loved the stories that connected the castle with Mary, Queen of Scots, who was a six day old baby when she came to the throne. It was in the castle that Mary gave birth to her son, who became James VI of Scotland and subsequently James I of Britain in 1603 when he united the crowns of Scotland and England.

Tragically, Mary had witnessed a savage murder at the Palace of Holyrood. Her husband Lord Darnley was jealous of Mary's friendship with her private secretary David Rizzio. One night Darnley, and a group of nobles, burst into the Queen's chambers and, in front of Mary, they brutally stabbed Rizzio to death.

Ruby was deep in daydreams and soon she was well behind the group. She was running to catch up when Ruby saw a woman, dressed in a dark, hooded coat, walking from the castle.

The woman hadn't noticed that a purse had fallen from her bag. Ruby tried to catch her attention but the woman was too preoccupied.

She picked up the heavy purse and shouted but the woman still didn't hear.

Ruby ran after her and tugged on her coat. The woman saw the girl holding out her purse, and she smiled and thanked Ruby.

'How kind. I would have been lost without this,' she said, grasping the purse. 'It contains everything that is important... precious... to me.'

Ruby noticed a sparkling ruby ring on the woman's hand as she took a shining object from the purse.

'Take this with my thanks. Hold it tightly. Look after it and it will look after you,' said the woman as she pushed the gift into Ruby's hand.

When Ruby opened her hand she saw a curious round object... silver and studded with jewels.

This was far too valuable. Ruby lifted her head to tell the woman she could not accept the gift.

But the woman had vanished. Ruby looked down towards the city but there was no sign of her. Ruby decided the best thing was to tell Miss Laird this strange story and ask her to take the shiny thing to the police station and hopefully have it returned to the woman.

As she approached the castle entrance she noticed a button on one side of the gift. She pressed it and the jewelled cover opened to reveal an old fashioned timepiece.

As Ruby walked into the castle she saw that the timepiece's hands were turning faster and faster... and going backwards!

Ruby gazed as the hands continued to spin backwards. She was aware that it had got darker and colder. Everything seemed... out of place.

The timepiece stopped spinning at three o'clock. Ruby was thinking about this when a shimmering light appeared in front of her. Through the glimmer there was a shadowy shape and a swooshing sound.

Ruby took a deep breath, gripped the timepiece and walked into the hazy light. As she got closer Ruby saw the shape was a beautiful lady dressed in a cloak that swept down to the ground.

Ruby gawped at this vision and realised she was breathing very quickly. She tried to compose herself and heard someone speak.

'Your Majesty, where are you? Call out, so we can find you.'

The lady in the cloak, who appeared to be floating over the ground, halted, raised a hand and replied... 'I am perfectly safe, ladies. Walk towards my voice.'

Four other figures appeared. They were also ladies, though their cloaks were not so grand, and they hurried towards the beautiful lady. They curtsied, all talking at once about how pleased they were to have found her.

'Thank goodness you are safe and well, Queen Mary,' said the tallest of the four ladies.

Ruby was astonished. For the past few weeks she had been preparing for the school test by studying the story of Mary, Queen of Scots.

Now she was standing opposite the legendary monarch and her ladies in waiting... Mary Fleming, Mary Seaton, Mary Livingston and Mary Beaton.

But how was that possible? These people lived in the 16th century... 500 years ago. As she wondered, Ruby saw the timepiece was giving off a bright light. Opening the cover, she saw that the time was still showing 3pm and the hands of the watch were throbbing.

'Three o'clock... 1500 hours,' thought Ruby. 'Amazing! The timepiece has taken me back to the 1500s when Mary ruled as Queen of Scots!'

This seemed crazy but there was no other explanation. Ruby was in Edinburgh Castle during the 16th Century as Mary, Queen of Scots, and her four Marys searched for something in the dimly lit corridors.

Then another thought struck her. Why had the Queen and her ladies in waiting not mentioned the girl wearing a crown who was standing in front of them?

Mary had seen Ruby at the castle entrance but deep within the castle walls she had become invisible to her and the Marys! Must be some kind of magic, Ruby thought, as she listened to them talking.

They were searching Edinburgh Castle for David Rizzio, the Queen's private secretary, who had been lured from the royal residence, the Palace of Holyroodhouse.

From her school work Ruby recalled that Rizzio was a singer and musician and that the Queen's fondness for him was to lead to Rizzio's murder.

Just as she had that memory, Ruby saw the Queen turn to the ladies...

'I am aware that some have plotted against David and it seems he has been kidnapped and held prisoner in the depths of the castle. Perhaps we should sing one of David's favourite songs. If he is in the castle he will hear us and respond,' said Queen Mary.

They started to sing as they walked along the dark corridor and Ruby followed. This process continued for quite some time. Occasionally the group would stop, cease singing and listen. But they heard nothing in response.

Then the Queen brought the parade to a sudden stop. 'Listen,' said Mary. 'I can hear a sound. It is very faint, but it is coming from down there.'

The Queen looked into the darkness and moved quickly as her ladies started to sing again.

Then, quite clearly, they heard a man's voice. Singing the same song as the women.

'It's coming from behind that door,' said Queen Mary, indicating a heavy, barred wooden door. 'Search for the key.'

The key hung on a hook on the wall. One of the ladies snatched it, inserted it in the lock and shoved the door.

In the half light they saw David Rizzio.

Rizzio bowed. 'Thank you, Your Majesty. I knew you would find me. Lord Darnley had me locked away for reasons that I do not understand.'

Mary, Queen of Scots, frowned. 'You are safe now and I will ask My Lord Darnley to explain himself. Now let us return to Holyrood for the evening meal.'

Mary, Queen of Scots, pointed the group away from the dungeon. As she did so, Ruby noticed the bright ring on the Queen's hand.

Where had she seen that before?

Ruby scratched her head... the penny dropped!

The mysterious woman had worn that ring. How could that be? Was she the ghost of Mary, Queen of Scots?

She wanted to warn Mary and her followers not to return to Holyrood because something terrible was going to happen to Rizzio. But they couldn't hear or see her. What could she do...

Ruby was deep in thought when she realised she was alone in the darkness. She looked at the glowing timepiece. Still showing 1500. Ruby pressed the button. The hands raced forward, followed by the swooshing sound and shimmering light.

Then there was the deafening bang of the One O'Clock Gun, traditionally fired each day at 1pm.

It was 1pm, obviously. But when Ruby looked again at the timepiece, the hands had stopped at 8pm!

She knew it was 1pm but according to the timepiece it was eight o'clock or 20:00 hours — the 2000s. Ruby was back in the present, at the entrance to Edinburgh Castle.

She saw Miss Laird and the other pupils. 'Oh, there is our Queen of the Castle,' said Miss Laird.

'Come along Queen Ruby. There's lots of wonders to see in Edinburgh Castle. Who knows we might even see one of the castle ghosts!'

Ruby smiled and nodded. Indeed, who knows, she thought.

EDINBURGH CASTLE

DID YOU KNOW?

The castle is Scotland's most popular tourist attraction, with more than *TWO MILLION* visiting in a year.

The rock on which Edinburgh Castle is built is prehistoric, estimated to be more than *350 MILLION YEARS OLD.*

The most tragic castle ghost is *THE GREY LADY,* said to be Janet Douglas, Lady of Glamis, who was executed after being accused of witchcraft.

The only monarch born at the castle was *JAMES VI* whose mother Mary, Queen of Scots gave birth to him there in 1566.